T0128563

A Different Life

Tonya J. Rodgers

authorHOUSE®

AuthorHouse™
1663 Liberty Drive
Bloomington, IN 47403
www.authorhouse.com
Phone: 1-800-839-8640

Published by AuthorHouse 2/20/2012

ISBN: 978-1-4678-3494-0 (e)
ISBN: 978-1-4678-3495-7 (sc)

Library of Congress Control Number: 2011919739

Chapter 1

"Run, Susie! Run! You can do it! Come On!

Susie was running for home plate. Her second homerun during the game. Finally, with the last of her energy, she slid into home. The game was won.

"Hooray for Susie! Hooray!"

"Susie, that was great! You are such a good baseball player. I hope we never lose you."

"I hope not either, Coach. I don't plan on going anywhere. I plan to be on the team as long as you will have me."

"Great! Hey, everyone! Let's go out for pizza to celebrate our win! My treat!"

"That sounds great, Coach!"

"Come on, Susie. You deserve a lot of credit for our win today. I'm delighted that you are part of our team. You are one heck of a player."

"Thanks, Coach. You know you are the one that taught me so much about baseball."

"Well, maybe so, but you are incredible out on the field. You are such a skilled player."

"I love baseball. What can I say? When I am on the field I feel on top of the world. It's a wonderful feeling. I hope I never have to give up that feeling."

"Let's hope not."

"Hey, kids, I want all of you to meet Mike. He is going to be helping me coach for a while. Mike knows a great deal about baseball as he has played the game since he was knee high. So I want all of you to welcome him and make him feel a part of the team."

"Hi, Mike!"

"Mike, I'd like for you to meet Susie. She is one of our best players."

"Hey. It's nice to meet you, Susie. I have heard a lot about you. I saw you at the game today and I can see what everyone is talking about. You are good."

"Well, thanks. I work really hard. The whole team does."

"Where do you go to school, Susie?"

"I'm a sophomore at Riverwood High. What about you?"

"I'm a junior at Eastmont. I live on the west side of town."

"I see. I didn't think I'd ever seen you at Riverwood. Are you playing on a team now or what?"

"No, not exactly. I played this spring with the school and then I had an ankle sprain. That's why I want to help out here for the summer. I've heard that your team is very good and even went to the play-offs last year. I hope we can all learn from each other."

"Well, then, I think it's going to be a great summer!"

"Hi, Susie!"

"Hey, Audrey. It's great to see you! Come on in. Boy, let me tell you something, girl."

"What is it, Susie?"

"I met this guy yesterday. He's going to help coach our baseball team this summer. He is soo cute and soo nice."

"Susie, you go girl. Maybe he'll ask you out."

"That would be great! But you know how I am. I'm so shy around boys."

"Susie, what do you mean? You underestimate yourself. You are so pretty. You can have any guy you want."

"Why aren't they flocking to my feet then? You know I'm not very popular."

"That doesn't matter. Apparently, you two have a lot in common since you are both baseball players. That should help. Just be yourself around him."

"Thanks for the tip, Audrey. You are such a good friend."

"You, too, Susie. Listen, I better be going. I've got to pick up some things for my mom at the store."

"I'm glad you stopped by."

"Me, too. I hope things go well for you and Mike."

"I hope so. Bye!"

Audrey! What a wonderful friend. She knew how to make people smile. When Susie was upset over something, Audrey could always make her feel better. For instance, the time Susie fell down the stairs at school and broke her leg. She had been so depressed staying in bed. But Audrey wouldn't hear of Susie feeling sorry for herself and she came while Susie's mother was at work and insisted they go shopping. She wouldn't take no for an answer. Audrey didn't mind having to help Susie as she did. She never minded doing anything for others. She was such a sweet and caring person. She would do anything for the people she cared about.

"Hi, Susie!"

"Hello, Mike. Where is everyone?"

"I guess they must be running late."

"Well, it is early on a Saturday morning."

"You're right, but I was up early. I was so excited to get here."

"Well, I almost overslept. I'm not used to getting up this early on Saturday mornings. Saturday's are my only chance to sleep a little later, but I guess not anymore now that I am helping coach you guys."

"You'll get used to it. I don't mind getting up early. I guess 'cause I enjoy baseball so much."

"I've noticed how much you seem to love it. You

seem to float from base to base when you're on the field and you're such a good player."

"I do enjoy softball. I feel great when I'm out there. I can't explain the feeling."

"That's wonderful!"

"It really is. I'm most happy when I'm playing softball."

"It certainly shows. This team is sure lucky to have you."

"Thanks."

"Mom, could I talk to you about something?"

"Sure, Honey."

"Well, there's this guy I like and he's just so great. He's nice and friendly to me and Mom, he's so gorgeous! I really, really like him. I would love to go out with him, but I'm not sure what to do. I don't know if he's interested in me. I mean, he talks to me and is very sweet, but I don't know if he would want to go out with me."

"Susie, my baby, you're growing up."

"I know that, Mom, and I'm scared of growing up. I really don't understand these feelings I'm having. Mike is great, and I really want to go out with him."

"Well, tell me about Mike."

"Oh, I didn't tell you already? He's our new assistant coach."

"Well, I guess I'll be seeing lots of him then at the games."

"You'd like him, Mom. You really would. I wish he was interested in me, too."

"How do you know he's not?"

"I guess I don't, but I don't have a lot of experience in the guy department."

"Susie, a lot of guys would enjoy going out with you. You're sweet, pretty, friendly, intelligent. I could go on and on. Susie, you're just like your father. If only he could be here to see how you've changed. You're not my little girl anymore. Susie, I love you, Honey, and I want you to come to me whenever you have a problem or concern. I'm always here for you."

"I will, Mom. I promise."

Chapter 2

"Good Morning, Mom. It's such a beautiful day!"

"Yes, it sure is, Susie. I love warm sunny mornings."

"Me, too. Oh, I'm excited this morning. I can't wait to get to baseball practice."

"I bet you're anxious to see Mike."

"Of course."

"What time is practice?"

"About nine. What time is it now?"

"Eight-thirty. Boy, you better hurry up if you're going to make it on time. Let me fix you a quick breakfast so you can get out of here. I've already started to put some bacon and toast on. Would that be okay?"

"Bacon and toast would be great! Thanks, Mom, you're the greatest! I love you."

"Gee, what brought that on?"

"Well, I don't always tell you how much I appreciate you. You do so much for me and I'm very grateful."

"I love you, too, Honey. I'm delighted you are in such a good mood. It wouldn't have something to do with Mike, would it?"

"Probably."

"Well, here's your toast and bacon. You better hurry up and eat, so you can get ready."

Susie hurriedly ate her breakfast and then scurried off to her room to put on her baseball uniform. Lying in her drawer, atop all her other clothes, she found her uniform. She always took great care with it and kept it neatly washed and ironed so that it would always be free of wrinkles. This was the beautiful blue and white uniform her father had bought for her. She remembered the first day she had worn it. She ran up to her father after the game, so excited that the team had won. He had been so proud of her. Susie had vowed that she would always do her best in everything because no matter what, she wanted him to be happy. She would never disappoint him.

"Bye, Mom! See ya later."

"Bye, Honey! Have fun at practice."

Susie ran out of the house. She was so excited to get to baseball practice today. She would get to see Mike. How great! She looked down at her watch to see what time it was. She didn't want to be late. 8:55! She quickly backed out into the street, without looking. A big truck was coming straight toward her, fast.

"Mom, Mom! Where am I? What's wrong? What happened? What happened, Mom?"

"Susie, you're okay, Honey. Calm down. Everything's okay."

"Where am I? What is going on, Mom?"

"Susie, you can't get too excited."

"If you don't tell me, I'll be worse. What's going on?"

"Susie. You were in an accident and you've been in the hospital for a few days, but you are going to be okay."

"What happened? What kind of an accident? I don't remember."

"Of course you don't. Just be thankful that you are now awake and you are okay. I have prayed so hard the last few days and God has answered my prayers."

"Tell me what happened, Mom!"

"You were in a car accident."

"A car accident? When?"

"Saturday morning."

"Oh, no. When I was going to baseball practice. Was I coming out of the driveway? That's the last thing I remember."

"You were backing out of the driveway."

"How horrible it must have been for me to end up like this! You've got to tell me all about it."

"Susie, you must not get upset."

"Well, I need to know what happened! It will drive

me crazy not knowing! I'm sorry for what you've gone through. Was it my fault, Mom?"

"Susie, why would you think a thing like that?"

"Well, I need to know. You're not telling me a whole lot so you must be keeping something from me."

"Oh, alright." As you were backing out of the driveway Saturday morning you hit an eighteen-wheeler truck."

"Oh, no! It was my fault! What could I have been thinking?"

"Susie, do you remember anything about it?"

"I'm not sure. I can't believe it! I didn't look back, Mom! I remember that I didn't look back! How could I have been so dumb? It's all my fault! Mom, I'm so sorry!"

"Honey, I'm just thankful you are okay. What we have to concentrate on now is getting you better so you can go home. I love you so much, Susie. You're alive, that's what's important. You're okay."

"Ms. Andrews, how is Susie doing?"

"Oh, Audrey, she's doing much better. She's going to be alright. She's been asking about you. I told her you came by to see her, but she doesn't remember anything from when she was in a coma. She would love to see you."

"She's really going to be okay, Ms. Andrews? I mean, the other day it really scared me seeing Susie like that, with tubes everywhere and not being able to wake up. I hated seeing her like that. It was like she was dying."

"I understand. I hated that, too, but she's much better now. She is alert and can talk to you."

"Okay, I'll try to go by to see her right away. Oh, Ms. Andrews, I'm delighted that she's alright. I don't know what I would have done if anything would have happened to her."

"Me, either. She means so much to so many people. She is so special."

"You are right, Ms. Andrews. Susie has certainly been a wonderful friend to me."

Chapter 3

"Hello, Susie! How's my best buddy doing?"

"Audrey! Oh, I'm so glad you're here."

"Can I get a great big hug from the great survivor?"

"You can get one from me, if that's who you mean."

"How are you feeling?"

"Okay, I guess, but I want to go home."

"I know. Maybe you won't be here much longer."

"I hope not."

"What's wrong, Susie? You don't sound too encouraging."

"Well, first of all I'm tired of laying here in this bed. The doctor has told me not to move around much, but that's hard to do, and he has told me that my legs are terribly bruised and that I shouldn't try to move them. The truth is, Audrey, I can't even feel my legs. It's like they are numb or something."

"Have you told the doctor this? Surely, they've done tests and all."

"Well, I haven't said anything. I have just done what he's told me to do. Maybe I'm just worried for nothing. I guess I should just listen to the doctor and not be so concerned. It's only been what, about a week, since my accident. Maybe my legs are just bruised and that's why I don't have any feeling in them."

"Have you tried moving them?"

"Yes, but I can't move them. The nurses have been coming in and turning me on my side and stuff. I haven't tried to get up and walk because the doctor told me it was too soon for that."

"Well, I'm sure if anything was wrong the doctor would have already told you. You need to concentrate on going home."

"I guess you're right, Audrey, I'm so sorry for what I've put everybody through. I can't stop thinking about the accident. Audrey, it was all my fault."

"You can't worry about that now. You are okay."

"It's not that easy. I have put a lot of people through unnecessary pain because of my carelessness."

"Things are going to happen in life, Suz, good and bad. Just consider yourself lucky. Accidents happen."

"But what if I hadn't been so lucky?"

"Susie, stop this! You are alive. You are okay. Life will go on. Yes, you had a serious car accident, but you can't change that now. You can't torture yourself for what could have happened."

"I know you're right, it's just going to take me a while

to get over this. Hey, I'm sorry, Audrey, about being such a drag."

"Don't apologize. You feel the way you feel."

"Thanks, Audrey. I'm glad you understand me the way you do. I really am glad to see you. I'm just tired of being here."

"You'll be going home soon, I'm sure. You seem to be doing okay so far."

"I guess so."

"You'll be out of here before you know it and back to playing baseball. Oh, and seeing Mike."

"That's right. I haven't even thought about him."

"I bet he has missed you."

"Oh, he probably hasn't even thought about me."

"Oh, I'm sure he has. He might even come to see you. Your mom said he called her the other day."

"Mom hasn't told me that. I can't believe she didn't tell me!"

"Your mother has had a lot on her mind. I'm sure she just forgot."

"Probably."

"Well, Suz, I hate to rush off, but when I came in the nurse said to keep the visit short so you can get your rest."

"Rest? I get all the rest I need. They won't let anyone stay too long."

"Hospital rules, I guess. But I promise I'll be back real soon."

"Thanks for coming. See ya later."

Chapter 4

"Doctor, are you sure Susie is paralyzed? She's never going to be able to use her legs again?"

"Ms. Andrews, I'm sorry."

"Is it permanent?"

"We're not sure. I think you should tell Susie as soon as possible. I've told her not to try to move her legs, but I know she probably is suspecting something is wrong. I didn't want to say anything until we performed more tests. We will try physical therapy in hopes that she may regain some use of her legs, but I don't know how successful that will be."

"There's no way the tests were wrong?"

"No, I'm afraid not, Ms. Andrews."

"How am I going to tell Susie?"

"Would you like for me to tell her?"

"Oh, no. I have to do it. It's going to be hard enough when she hears it from me."

"Ms. Andrews, I'm terribly sorry about this. I know this must be horrible news, but it'll be okay."

"Thank you, Doctor. I'm just worried about Susie. This news is going to ruin her life. I just know it."

How was she going to tell Susie about this? How would she react? No more baseball. Susie would rather die than live and not be able to ever play baseball again. She had already been through enough in her lifetime. When her father died it took her a long time to get over it, and she still had nightmares. She had just started being happy again.

"Hi, Susie. Are you feeling okay?"

"Hi, Mom. What are you doing here so soon? I wasn't expecting you till later."

"Well, your doctor called and wanted to talk to me."

"Great! I hope it was about me going home."

"Not quite. Honey, I have something to tell you."

"What is it, Mom? You sound like it's very important."

"It is. Honey, you know you have been telling me you can't move your legs and the feel numb? Well, Dr. Norman just got some test results back. It seems as if you have a spinal cord injury and are paralyzed from waist down."

"What are you talking about? They said I would be okay. I trusted the doctors. They don't know. I can move them. I know I can. I just haven't been trying because they told me not to."

"Susie, it's okay."

Susie removed the sheets and tried to bend her legs at the knee. Nothing happened.

"I can't be paralyzed! I just can't!"

"Honey, I know. I wish there was something I could do."

"Is this permanent?"

"Well, you will receive physical therapy to help strengthen your muscles and all, but Dr. Norman says he doesn't know for sure if it's permanent or not. I wish I knew, but regardless we will deal with this."

"I could be like this forever? Why is this happening to me? I'm so confused! Being paralyzed has got to be the worst thing! What am I going to do?"

"First of all, you're going to concentrate on getting well so you can go home."

"What do you mean by getting well? I'll never be totally well again."

"Susie, don't talk like that."

KNOCK! KNOCK! A sound at the door. Who could that be? Susie certainly didn't want to talk to anyone right now. The door slowly opened.

"Hello Can I come in?"

It was Mike.

"Sure, come on in", replied Susie's mother.

"Hi, Susie. How are you?"

"I'm okay. Mike, you haven't met my mom, have you?"

"No, I haven't."

"Hi, Mike, nice to meet you"

"You, too. Susie's told me a lot about you."

"I'm sure of that. Well, I'm going to leave you two to talk, if that's alright, Susie. If you need anything I'll be downstairs in the cafeteria."

"Mom, go home and get some rest. I'll call if I need anything."

"Are you sure? I hate to leave you like this."

"I'll be alright, Mom. Thanks, Mom."

"Alright then, but you call me or I'll call you. I'll be back later."

"Bye, Mom."

"Bye, kids."

"Susie, did I come at a bad time?"

"No, Mike. I'm glad you came. Sorry, I'm a little upset. I hate for you to see me like this."

"That's okay. I'm sure you're ready to go home. We've all been very worried about you, Susie."

"That's what I've heard. I really miss everybody."

"We miss you, too. We're so glad you're okay."

"Have you missed me, too?"

"Of course. When are you going home?"

"I don't know. Soon, I hope."

"I'm sure you can't wait to get back to playing baseball."

Oh, No! Why did he have to say that? She would never be able to play baseball in this condition. Oh, boy! This was going to be harder than she thought. Tears began streaming down Susie's face. Oh, she hadn't wanted Mike to know about her pain.

"Susie, are you okay?"

"Sure. It's just that it's going to be a while before I can play baseball again and I miss it so."

"I understand that. You've been through a terrible ordeal."

"Oh, Mike. It's so hard. Being in this hospital, not being able to play baseball. I just hat it so."

"Susie, you'll be back playing in no time."

"Honestly, I don't know, Mike. I'm paralyzed. I can't walk. I don't know if I will ever walk again."

"What do you mean? I thought everything was okay."

"Well, it's not. It will never be okay. My Mom just told me. That's what we were talking about when you came in."

Mike looked down at his watch. He had to leave. He just couldn't handle this right now.

"Um, Susie, I hate to do this, but I have to leave. There's someplace I need to be and I'll be late if I don't get going. Sorry."

Mike walked out the door, hurriedly.

"Mike, Mike..."

He was gone and Susie hadn't even said goodbye.

"Welcome Home, Susie!"

"Audrey, what are you doing here?"

"Isn't it obvious? I came to welcome you home."

"Oh, isn't that nice. Well, you can go because I don't want you here."

"What do you mean? I came to see you."

"Where have you been for the last week? Since I found out I am paralyzed you didn't bother to stop by and see me. Were you afraid to come see a paralyzed girl?"

"I was afraid. I didn't know what I would say. Susie, you are my best friend and it hurt me to know you were hurting."

"Why are you here now?"

"I realized that I had to get over my fear. I had to see you. I'm sorry that I didn't come to see you after I found out about your paralysis, but I was so shook up about it. I didn't want to upset you, too."

"Audrey, I'm so disappointed in you. You have been my best friend forever. You couldn't have upset me anymore than I already was. You know that."

"Susie, I was scared."

"Audrey, I don't want to deal with this right now. Please just leave."

"Susie, you have to understand."

"I do understand, Audrey. You don't really care about me. When I needed you the most you weren't there."

"Oh, Susie, I hate that you feel that way because that's simply not true."

"Just leave, Audrey. I can't handle this. Let me have some peace for a while."

"Okay, if that's what you want. Bye, Suz."

Audrey left with tears streaming down her face, upset that her friendship with Susie might be over.

Chapter 5

June 15th was Susie's birthday. She was real excited! She and her mother were going out to the country. It was certainly a lovely day! When they arrived in the country they picked a beautiful spot by the lake so they could eat.

"Mom, thanks for bringing me out here today. Being here makes me realize how lucky I am to be alive."

"You are very fortunate, Susie."

"It's hard for me to count my blessings, ya know? I mean, even though, I suppose, there are still many things I can do, I seem to want to dwell on what I can't do."

"You can't keep doing that, Susie. You have to concentrate on other things. We all take our legs for granted, but, Honey, just because you can't use yours anymore doesn't mean that your life is over."

"That's true, I guess, but all I think about is not being able to walk. How can I think about anything else?"

"You have to get out more, Susie. And most of

all, you should be with those who love you and care about you."

"I guess you're talking about Audrey."

"Yes, I am. She was terribly hurt by what you said to her when you came home from the hospital. Maybe you should go visit her. It's been quite a while."

"Mom, I'm still upset. I can't understand why she didn't come see me. Audrey had nothing to be afraid of. I needed her."

"Susie, just stop for a moment and think about someone besides yourself. When Audrey heard about your accident she was horrified. She thought she was going to lose her best friend. Susie, you two are like sisters. Then she came to see you when you were unconscious and seeing you with all those tubes around you frightened her even more. It took a lot of courage for her to come see you after you got better. And when I called her and told her you were paralyzed she was almost destroyed. I don't' think you really have any idea how much she cares about you, Susie."

"But I needed her then, Mom."

"She came to see you when you came home. She was there for you then and she could have been here for you for the past couple of weeks, too, if you wouldn't have been so hard on her. "

"I don't know."

"You've always been stubborn, Susie, but remember, Audrey is your best friend, and I know I wouldn't let something like this destroy your friendship."

"Maybe you're right. I do love Audrey. She's just like family. I've really missed her."

"Then do something about it, Susie. Do something now, before it's too late."

"Hi, Susie. It's good to see you here."

"Hi, Coach. I had to come to see you guys."

"Susie, I'm really sorry about everything, but you are always going to be a member of the team. Without you, we wouldn't be where we are today."

"You know how to cheer me up. Thanks, Coach. I just wish I could be out there with everyone else. I feel totally lost without baseball. It really feels strange sitting here. I would give anything to be able to walk out on that field."

"Everything will be okay, Susie."

"Everybody keeps saying that to me. Boy, I wish I could go back to that morning of the accident. It was all my fault, ya know? Now God has punished me. That's what this is all about. I was careless."

"Susie, don't say that. It was a freak accident."

"Well, whatever. I don't understand why it had to happen to me, though. Without baseball I feel my life is completely empty."

"Things will get better. Just give it time."

"I don't know if time will help. I think every night before I go to bed that the next day will be better, but it seems like it's harder."

"Obviously not, Susie, because it took a lot of courage for you to come here today."

"I don't think I'd call it courage. I felt like I needed to come. I can't explain it. I thought that if I could see the team play today then maybe I wouldn't feel so empty. It's really weird."

"No, not really."

Just then Mike approached Susie and her coach. Oh, she was so glad to see him. Maybe they could talk for a while, if he had time.

"Coach, sorry to interrupt, but Tommy needs to talk to you before the game."

"Thanks, Mike. Susie, we'll talk later."

"Good luck with the game!"

"Hi, Susie. How are you?"

"I'm fine, Mike. It's good seeing you again. Mike....."

Susie wasn't quite sure what she should say next.

"Susie, it's really good to see you here."

"Thanks, I'm glad I came."

"So, um, what have you been up to lately?"

It appeared as though it was difficult for Mike to talk to Susie.

"Truthfully? Nothing, really. I can't really do much of anything. I just sit at home waiting and hoping someone might drop by to see me. I get so bored and lonely."

"I'm sorry."

"Don't be. That's just the way it is."

"It'll get better."

"I'm tired of everyone saying that. You can't imagine how hard it is for me to get through everyday without thinking how horrible my life is. Everyone wants to ignore the reality of the situation. And you, well, when you found out I was paralyzed you ran away in fear. Well, how do you think I feel having to deal with all of this? No one knows what I'm going through."

"Susie, I'm sorry about running out, but I explained why."

"Of course, you made up some crummy excuse. Just be honest, Mike, you couldn't handle it. But what I don't understand is why it upset you so much."

"No, you've got it all wrong."

"Whatever, it doesn't matter."

"Yes, it does to me, Susie!"

Mike's voice got deeper and louder.

"Mike, you don't have to get so defensive. It's okay."

"I had to get to practice that day! I was running late!"

"Mike, why are you acting like this? I said it's okay."

"It's just that I kind of understand what you're going through"

"What do you mean?"

"Never mind,Susie. I shouldn't have said anything."

"Mike, you started it. Tell me what you're talking about."

"It's just that my older sister was paralyzed in a tragic accident several years ago. She was paralyzed from her neck down. She could only move her head."

"Oh, I don't know what to say, Mike. I had no idea."

"Of course you didn't'. Just forget it. I don't want you to feel worse because of this."

"How is she now?"

"Well, that's just the thing. She didn't make it. She committed suicide shortly after her accident."

"Oh, Mike. I'm so sorry. It must be hard for you to talk about it."

"Sort of. That's something you never get over. When you told me you were paralyzed it just brought back a lot of bad memories. I didn't mean to upset you."

"I understand now. It's okay. I'm just sorry that I had to remind you of a terrible situation."

"It's not your fault. Maybe it's good that I though about it again."

"Why do you say that? It has to really hurt to remember."

"I try to remember the good things about my sister. Sometimes it helps just to talk to someone."

"Maybe, but most people don't understand what I'm going through."

"Maybe if you would just try. My sister would never even give people a chance to understand. She was so miserable."

"Oh, I can't even imagine what she went through. Being paralyzed from my waist down is hard enough. I can't imagine being paralyzed from the neck down. She really couldn't do anything, could she?"

"No, she couldn't. She led a very active lifestyle

before her accident and it just killed her that she couldn't do anything. She thought there was no other way out. She couldn't do anything. I know this sounds horrible, but maybe she did the right thing for her situation. The doctors gave her very little hope of recovering. She was young and had most of her life ahead oh her to be paralyzed like that. Susie, you can still do a lot. You still have your upper body and your arms and hands. Don't become depressed like my sister and feel you have no way out."

"I am trying, but it is very hard not to."

"Susie, what are you doing after the game?"

"Going home, I guess."

"Would you like to grab a bite to eat and maybe we could talk about things?"

"I don't know, Mike."

"Why not? I think we both could lean on one another for a while. I'm a real good listener."

"Well, I suppose I can't say no to that. I could use a friend right now."

"Great! Oh, well, I better go before they start calling for me. The game's about to start. I'll see you a little later."

"Hi, Audrey! May I come in?"

Susie had finally decided to visit with Audrey.

"Susie, I'm pretty busy."

"Please, Audrey. I think we need to talk."

"Come on in."

Susie came in, as Audrey closed the door behind her. Boy, it had really be a long time since she'd been here. She'd really missed coming over all the time.

"What do you want to talk about?"

"First of all, I want to apologize for the way I acted when I came home from the hospital. I didn't know what I was saying. I was angry and upset. Not just at you, but at everything. You're my best friend and I don't want our friendship to end. You're important to me and I want you to understand how I'm feeling."

"I think you've already made it clear how you feel. You didn't' try to understand what I was feeling. Susie, I love you, just like my own flesh and blood. I was hurting, too."

"I'm so sorry about that."

"Susie, I've always tried to be there for you when you needed me, but I was so confused myself. I thought you would have understood that."

"Audrey, I was devastated at the time. You don't know how painful it has been for me."

"Yes, I do know. I've been feeling that same pain for weeks now."

"Audrey, I don't know what to say, except that I'm sorry. I've missed you so much. I really could have used your sense of humor over the past couple of weeks. I realize now that I'm to blame for you not being there. Maybe I have been selfish about all of this. Please forgive me. You are my best friend and I don't want to lose you."

"Oh, Suz, I don't want to lose your friendship, either. I'm really sorry for everything, too. I'm sorry I hurt you."

"Audrey, let's just start fresh. I need you now more than ever. You really mean a lot to me."

"I'm really glad you came over, Suz. I've been miserable lately without you around. You are the best and I love you."

"And I love you, too, Sis."

"Hi, Susie."

"Hi, Mike. What a surprise seeing you here." Susie had just sat down to grab a bite to eat at Manno's Restaurant, located right next to the baseball field.

"Susie, are you eating all alone?"

"Yes. I wanted to be alone for a while. I haven't been good company for the past few days."

"What's wrong?"

"Just feeling all down and out. I can't seem to do anything but feel sorry for myself. But anyway, what are you doing here?"

"I just dropped by to get a snack before practice."

"I see. I wish I could join you."

"Susie, maybe you should try to get out more. Maybe that would help. Just because you can't use your legs, doesn't mean that the rest of you is paralyzed, too. Come on. You can do so much more than you think."

"You're just saying that, Mike."

"No, I mean it. You have to stop dwelling on what

you can't do because you are so wonderful and can do anything you set your mind to."

"I used to think I could, but I'm not so sure anymore. I'm so different now. I'm filled with anger and confusion. I feel like such a horrible person."

"Susie, that's understandable. You've been through a terrible ordeal and of course you feel cheated. But you can't let that destroy who you really are. My sister felt like such a burden to everyone, but what she wouldn't allow herself to see was how much joy she gave my family. I couldn't help her, Susie, so give me a chance to help you. I'm here for you if you ever need someone to talk to."

"Thanks, Mike. That means a lot to me."

"I just think you're someone special."

"You are, too."

"Susie, there's something I've been wanting to ask you, but with everything you've been through lately, well, I though I better wait. Would you like to go out with me?"

"You mean, like a date?"

"Exactly."

"Gee, I don't know. Are you sure?"

"Of course. I really like you, Susie."

"That would be great!"

"I'm glad you agree. I really want to get to know you better."

"Mike, you're incredible! It doesn't bother you that

I'm in a wheelchair? You're not afraid to be seen with me?"

"Of course not, Susie."

"Mike, you make me feel really special. Thanks."

Chapter 6

"Audrey, should I wear this pink dress or the yellow one, or maybe I should wear jeans? I don't know! Help!"

"Susie, please calm down! I know this is you first date with Mike, but you can't get hysterical."

"I can't help it. I'm so excited! Oh, Audrey, what should I wear?"

"I think jeans would be good. Those black jeans and that purple blouse would look great together!"

Susie was so nervous. Her first date with Mike! Mike was so cute! And so sweet! Ding! Ding! It was the doorbell. Mike was here.

"Hi, Susie. Wow, you look great!"

"Thanks. You, too."

Susie could barely speak. Mike almost took her breath away. Usually, she saw him in practice clothes, but now he was all cleaned up and looked different than Susie had ever seen him.

"Hey, kids! Hi, Mike," Susie's mother came walking towards the door. "How are you doing? It's nice to see you again."

"Hey, Ms. Andrews. It's nice to see you, too."

"Where are you two going?"

"Well, it's sort of a surprise, Ms. Andrews."

"I see. Well, have lots of fun. But, Mike, you take care of my baby, okay?"

"Mom!"

"Susie, I'm serious. Mike understands."

"Of course I do, Ms. Andrews. I'll take good care of Susie."

"I know you will, Mike. Don't be out too late."

"Alright, Mom. Bye!"

"Bye, Kids!"

"Are you as nervous as I am?" asked Mike, after they both got in the car.

"I sure am," replied Susie, "But, Mike, you are so very different from most other guys. I'm so glad I met you. You are a lot like me. I really believe you can relate to what I'm going through. I feel like I can talk to you about what I'm feeling and you understand. You don't know how comforting that is to me."

"Susie, you don't have to be alone. I'm glad that you feel that way about me because I do want to help you. But you know another thing? You seem to understand me, too. You are so easy to talk to. I feel I can tell you anything."

"Me, too. No one can understand what I'm feeling and you seem to be the closest one who can relate to my situation. So many people try to help me and try to understand, but they can't."

"Well, Susie, I'm here for you whenever you need me. I still have a lot of painful memories of my sister's ordeal and talking to you seems to make things easier. I really enjoy being with you. I hope we can become good friends."

"Mike, you're so wonderful! Thanks for caring. It means a lot to me."

"I just want to help. I think that if I can help then it's like helping my sister. I know that probably doesn't make a whole lot of sense, but I feel so guilty for what happened to her."

"Why do you feel guilty?"

"Like I didn't do enough. It hurt me to see her suffering, but she would never talk to me. If she would have told me what was going on inside maybe she would still be alive today."

"You can't think that. It's not your fault. I'm sure you did everything you could."

"No, I don't think I did. If only we'd known what she was planning to do, maybe then we could have done something, anything to stop her."

"Mike, it's over. You can't go back. My God, listen to me. Here I am telling you that you can't keep reliving the past, and that's what I seem to keep doing. I keep thinking that if only I could go back to that morning of the accident and have been more careful. What if? What if? But it's too late now. No matter how hard it is, I guess I have to carry on. Of course, that's easier said than done."

"It sure is, but I think that it will get easier for you. You're still alive, Susie. You have a chance to live a full life. Don't destroy that chance."

"I know that, I think. It's just hard to explain how I feel right now. Do you know how difficult it is to hear that you are paralyzed? That you may never walk again? That morning my mom told me, I was in total disbelief. I knew she had to be wrong, even though I knew she was right."

"Susie, I'm glad you can share your feelings with me. I just hope you have a good time tonight. I want things to be perfect."

"Oh, they are perfect, Mike. So far I'm having a terrific time. Just being around you, talking to you, is great. I'm really happy you asked me out. I think God sent you to me, Mike, to help me."

"Me, too. You're really special, Susie. I hope you realize that. God is keeping a close eye on you, so don't disappoint Him and don't disappoint yourself, either. Too many people care about you to see you hurt."

Chapter 7

Days went by so slowly now. Susie began to get quite lonesome. Most of the kids were at the swimming pool or on vacation. Susie sat at home and watched television. Once a week she continued her visits to the physical therapist, although each session became harder and harder. She wanted to walk again, but she wasn't sure she could keep suffering like she was now. Ring! Ring! The telephone. Susie wondered who it could be. She thought she was the only person within miles who would be home on such a gorgeous summer afternoon. Anyway, Susie slowly wheeled to the phone, feeling sure it was for her mother who was working.

"Hi, Suz. What are you doing? You want to go shopping?" Audrey was calling.

"Hi, Audrey. Sure, I'd love to go."

"Great! We haven't been shopping in such a long time and I thought it would be fun."

"Sounds like fun."

"Okay. I'll be over in a bit."

"Bye. And Audrey, thanks."

"Sure."

"Audrey, I've had a wonderful time today. I just love shopping with you. My mother is going to kill me when she finds out what I bought. I forgot how fun shopping could be. It was a little difficult at times having to wheel myself around, but I really didn't mind that much."

"I had fun, too, Susie. We have to do things like that more often. I'm sorry we haven't had a chance to get together lately, but I promise from now on we'll make time to have fun together. Well, are you ready to order?"

Susie and Audrey had stopped by a local restaurant for lunch.

"Not yet. Everything looks so good, it's hard to choose."

"I know what you mean. Oh, Suz, look who's over there. Isn't that Mike?"

"Where?"

"Right over there. Don't you see him? Who is that he's with? Is that his sister?"

"He doesn't have a sister anymore."

"Oh, must be a friend or something."

"Oh, Audrey, they're leaving and coming straight this way!"

"Hey, Susie. Hey, Audrey," Mike greeted them. " What are you two up to?"

"Eating, obviously. Who is your friend?"

"Susie, Audrey, this is Meredith. Meredith, this is Audrey and Susie."

"Nice to meet you, Meredith. You're very pretty. How do you two know each other?"

"We're good friends."

"I see. Well, you two have fun."

"Thanks, you too."

"Boy, Audrey, that guy has some nerve. What kind of game is he playing? I thought he was interested in me. I guess he just felt sorry for me."

"Susie, don't jump to conclusions. She said they were friends."

"I don't believe that. Audrey, do you mind if we get out of here? I don't feel too good. I can't believe Mike would do this to me."

"Susie, you are getting carried away. They were just having lunch together. What's wrong with him having lunch with a friend. Aren't you guys just friends? You act as if he is all yours."

"I just thought he cared about me. I want to go home."

Audrey took Susie home, even before they were able to order any food. It was no use arguing with Susie. Audrey had seen nothing wrong with Mike having lunch with a female friend, but all Susie could see was that he was having lunch with a girl, a very pretty girl, and Susie was jealous and upset.

"Susie, can I come in?"

"Mom, I'd like to be alone, please."

"What's wrong, Honey? You've been in your room since I came home from work."

"I'm okay. I'm just tired after shopping today. That's all."

"Susie, I think it's more than that. You wouldn't eat supper. Did something happen today?"

"No, I told you I'm just tired. Please stop bugging me. I don't feel well."

"Alright, Honey. I'll leave you alone for now, but you have to come out of this room some time. I know something is upsetting you, but I won't pressure you to tell me what it is."

"Thanks, Mom."

Boy, how could she tell anybody what happened, Susie thought. Mike had humiliated her. Everyone would feel sorry for her now if they knew what he had done. How could he? She had thought that he really understood because of his sister's ordeal. Obviously, she had been mistaken.

"Hey, Suz, how about lunch today?"

"You mean it, Audrey? I need to get out."

"Great! Let's go somewhere different."

"That sounds lovely! Any place where I won't possibly run into Mike."

"Susie, how are you doing about that? This is the first time you've mentioned him in the past few days."

"I'm not concerned about him anymore. I'm sorry I brought up his name."

"He hasn't been to see you?"

"No, and I don't want him to. I need to concentrate only on walking again. I don't have time to worry about Mike."

"Susie, your mother called me yesterday. She was really worried about you. I know you're hurt and I don't want you to keep it inside. You can talk to me. Please talk to me. I think you're trying to cover up how you really feel."

"Audrey, do you have to ruin this wonderful day for me? I don't want to talk about it."

"Alright, but I just want you to know that it's okay. I want to help if I can."

"I know."

"Well, where do you want to eat?"

"It doesn't matter, just as long as I'm with the greatest friend in the world."

"No, you're the greatest, Susie. Remember that."

Later that evening, Susie was sitting on the front porch and a car drove up in the driveway. A familiar car and a familiar face.

"Hi, Susie. How are you doing?"

"Fine, I guess."

"It's a beautiful day, isn't it? Mind if I have a seat?"

"Suit yourself."

"What have you been doing lately?"

"Nothing, really."

"I've been meaning to call you, but I've been sort of busy."

"That's okay."

"I've missed you, though."

"Mike, what did you come by for? I'm not in the mood for small talk. If you came by to see me, okay. Say what you need to say and leave."

"Why are you acting so mean?"

"Mike, I'm not stupid. I know why you haven't called me. You are seeing someone else."

"No, I'm not. That girl you saw me with the other day is just a friend."

"Is that what you tell everybody about us? That we're just friends. That Susie Andrews is a poor, helpless cripple who needs as many friends as she can get right now."

"Susie, you know I would never say something like that."

"How do I know you wouldn't? You told me that you didn't date much, and it just so happens that right after our first date I see you with another girl. Oh, but I guess I have no hold on you. I mean, we just went on one date. That doesn't really mean anything. I guess not to you, anyhow. I just trusted you, that's all."

"Susie, I'm sorry. I do care for you. Meredith and I are only friends. She just asked me to go to lunch with her. That's it."

"You don't have to explain it to me."

"Yes, I do. I wasn't quite sure if I should go because of you, but I really thought there was no harm in it. The whole time I was with Meredith, I kept wishing I was with you."

"Mike, it's okay. You don't have to try to cheer me up. You don't owe me anything. I 'm just sorry that all you feel for me is pity."

"You think I feel sorry for you? That's the last thing I feel. You seem to be doing a good enough job of that yourself."

"Mike, you don't understand. You're just like everyone else, aren't you? People think that because I'm paralyzed that I'm supposed to get special attention. Yes, attention is nice, but I don't want anyone's sympathy. A lot of people see me differently because I'm paralyzed. They don't think that I'm normal. When we went out and you proved to me that you didn't mind being seen in public with me, well, that made me feel proud. It felt good. And when I saw you with another girl, all I could see was how normal she was. She was so pretty and she could walk, and I can't compete with someone like that."

"Susie, you don't have to compete. You're wonderful in your own special way. I really hate this had to happen. You were just beginning to trust me, and I messed it up. I'm really sorry, but you have got to stop having a pity party."

"Mike, I don't want to get hurt again. I have suffered through so much in the past few months and I can't take anymore. I have to concentrate on walking again. That is the only thing that's important to me now."

"Susie, I'm sorry you're hurting. Come on, why don't you come to dinner with me tonight?"

"Are you kidding? Do you think I can just get over what happened?"

"Susie, I care about you. I can't just forget about you. You're very special to me. The first time I saw you I knew you were special, and I couldn't wait to meet you. You stood a part from everyone else on that baseball field. You seemed incredible. I knew at that moment that you were someone I wanted to know."

"Mike, I care about you a great deal, too, but I have other things to concentrate on right now. I have to get a lot of things straightened out before we can start over. Maybe this all seems ridiculous to you. You're probably wondering why I've gotten so carried away with what happened. I'm sure it seems like a small issue to you, but to me it's the main issue in my life."

"I want you to be happy, Susie."

"Me, too."

"Well, I guess I should be going then."

"Good-bye, Mike. See you around."

Mike left, obviously feeling very upset. Susie, on the other hand, was confused. She wanted to trust Mike, but should she? She felt she couldn't take the risk of being hurt this way again.

Chapter 8

The following Tuesday, Susie awoke with a strange feeling. It really frightened her. Somehow she felt as though something horrible was going to occur, so she slowly crawled out of bed and reached for her wheelchair. As she lifted herself up, she fell.

"Mom!" She shouted.

"What's wrong, Susie?" Her mother came rushing into the room. "Oh, Honey, what happened?"

"Something's wrong, Mom."

"Here, let me help you."

"Mom, you have to get me to the doctor."

"Honey, it's okay. You just fell."

"I want to see the doctor, Mom. Please call him."

"Okay, Susie, if you feel strongly about it. Let me help you get dressed and then I'll go call him."

"No, go ahead. I think I can manage."

Susie's mother called the doctor and was told to

bring Susie right to his office. The doctor examined Susie and told her everything was okay. She seemed to be making some progress in therapy and he felt she should continue with this. He told her that perhaps she just lost her upper body strength temporarily this morning, but that it was nothing to be concerned about. Susie, however, was visibly upset. Falling this morning really made her see that walking again may not happen. She was so sick of being this way. For months now she'd been on an emotional rollercoaster. One minute she was happy and thought that everything was going to be okay, but the next minute something would go wrong and she'd wish she was dead. Should she even continue trying to walk again?

"Hi, Susie. Are you okay?" Audrey came by to check on her friend.

"I don't know, Audrey. I'm just so tired of feeling miserable. I think God must be punishing me."

"Susie, don't say that. We have to think of all this as part of God's will."

"I don't know. I wish I could accept that as an answer, but that's really no consolation. I just can't believe God would let all this happen to me."

"Maybe there's a purpose in all of this."

"I wish I could see it. I just don't have the faith in Him as I once did, before all this happened."

"You're just doubting what has happened to you. You're questioning His ways. It's only normal, Susie, but you can't let it destroy your faith in Him. He does what is best for us. You have to let Him help you through this ordeal."

"But how? I've been out of touch with Him for a long time."

"Just allow Him back into your life."

"I'm just so confused, Audrey. I'm not sure anyone can help me right now. I feel like just giving up."

"Susie, don't say that. You have so much ahead of you."

"I can see nothing for me, Audrey. My future looks like total darkness. I have nothing to live for."

"Susie, you have so many people who love you. Let us help. Let God help."

"I don't know if I can. I feel like this is all my fault. It is all my fault. I'm the one who had the accident. I caused it."

"Susie, stop feeling guilty. That is only hurting you now. You can only look ahead, not behind you."

"How can I? I can't forget about my paralysis. That is a part of my past, my present, and my future."

"Then accept it. You're going to have to come to terms with it sooner or later. I don't think you ever have come to terms with it. You have blocked out the fact that you might be paralyzed for the rest of your life."

"You don't have any idea how hard that is to accept! You don't have to live with the fact of never walking or running again. It's torture!"

"Susie, what is easy in life? If nothing was ever

difficult in life, we wouldn't be here today. You need to turn to someone, Suz. Come on. I want to take you somewhere."

"Audrey, I really don't feel like going anywhere."

"Susie, don't argue with me. You're going whether I have to drag you or not."

"Fine. But where are you taking me?"

"Some place you've needed to go for some time. A place that's really going to give you comfort."

Audrey insisted that Susie go with her. They finally got into the car and drove several blocks. They stopped in front of one of the biggest churches in the area. One that Susie and her mother and father used to attend regularly.

"Audrey, Church?"

"Yes, Susie. How long has it been since you were here?"

"I can't remember. I guess not since my dad died. We all used to come here a lot when he was alive, but after his death, Mom and I just never came back."

"Well, I'm glad I brought you then."

"Audrey, you expect me to go inside and pray? How can I pray when I am doubting God?"

"Susie, you can pray to God that He will help you understand and stop doubting Him. You need Him. Now I'm going to be in the back. Take your time. No one else is here, so just feel comfortable."

"Audrey, thanks. I'm not quite sure that this is the answer, but I'm going to try. I just hope He'll listen."

"He will."

Susie wheeled herself up to the altar which was quite a distance from the entrance. She gently lifted her head as she looked at a picture of Jesus on the center of the wall.

"Dear Lord, I haven't prayed to you in such a long time. I guess this is actually kind of strange. I didn't even want to come here, but my best friend, Audrey, brought me anyway. I was surprised when she pulled up here. I guess it sort of brought back a lot of memories from when I was younger. My mom, dad, and I used to come here almost every Sunday. I really don't know what happened. My dad died and my mom and I just stopped coming. Audrey says You can help me, that you can give me some comfort. I'm not sure, but I'm willing to try anything. I really do need someone that understands. Maybe You can help. I'm just so angry right now. I want to blame what has happened to me on someone else. It seems so unfair that I have to be the one who may never be able to use my legs again. I keep asking myself – why me? Why me, Lord? You know I'm not a strong person. Everyone keeps telling me that I am, but I'm not. I've tried to appear okay to everyone, but that's not working too well. I need something to grasp onto. I don't know where I'm headed. I have no direction. I feel my life has come to an end. In several weeks I'm going back to school. I'm terrified of going back. It will be so different than before. I need your help in guiding me, Lord. My life feels so empty. I am lucky that I have had such good friends and family to support me and be there when I need them, but none of them really understand what I'm going through. How could they? No one can know the kind of torture that I suffer through unless they've experienced this type of paralysis. Even going to the bathroom is a nightmare. Everything that I do is a big task now. I have to use other parts of my body to make up for the legs I can't use. Try getting on a toilet without using your legs. It's not very pleasant. Oh, and let's not forget Mike. He seemed to be the one that came closest to understanding my ordeal. At first, Lord I thought You brought him into my life to help me, but he ended up hurting me. I don't understand that. Was he brought into my life for a purpose? I don't know. I suppose if he was, well, I destroyed it. I thought at first that he could help me because of the situation with his sister, but then I saw him with another girl and I blew everything out of proportion. I was so hurt. Don't You understand, Dear Lord? I didn't want to think that he could hurt me. I trusted him. I mean really trusted him and he destroyed that. You don't know how difficult it has been lately for me to trust anyone. I think that most people just feel sorry for me. Maybe everyone doesn't feel that way, but it's so hard for me to believe that anyone just wants to help me, Susie Andrews. I see them as wanting to help a crippled, helpless girl. Lord, please help me to let other people help me. Dear Lord, help me to understand what has happened. Guide me in the right direction, Lord. I'm sorry for doubting you, but you must understand that my life before the accident was baseball. My father taught me how to play when I was a little kid and playing baseball helped keep a part of him with me. When I lost him, I lost a big part of me. Baseball allowed me to remember him and keep him in my heart always. I felt that if I played baseball I would keep his memories with me. Maybe that's why I was such a good player because I wanted so bad not to forget him. I remember running so fast because I felt that the faster I ran the harder it would be for me to forget him. Yes, I enjoyed baseball, but I wasn't just playing for myself. I was playing for my dad. My father meant so much to me. Since the accident I guess I have learned that he will always be with me. I am a part of him. I guess I don't need baseball to keep him with me. Lord, thanks for listening. Please continue to help me. I have a long road ahead of me and I need strength and courage to get me through."

"Hi, Susie. How are you feeling this morning?"

"Alright, I guess, Mom."

"Well, good. Remember, we're having dinner with Ted tonight?"

"Oh, I forgot. Does it have to be tonight.? I'm not sure I feel like being in public."

"Come on, Susie. I want you to meet Ted. I want you to get to know him. Besides, I think you need to get out."

"Okay, I suppose you're right."

"Thanks, Susie. This is very important to me. I really like Ted and I think you will, too."

"Mom, I said I would meet him. Don't expect me to like him the first time I see him."

"Susie, just give it a try, give Ted a chance."

"Oh, Mom. There you go again trying to make everything so "wonderful" again. I have so much else in my life to worry about now than worrying about your new boyfriend."

"Susie, I have been trying so hard to help you. You need to help yourself. I'm sick of you feeling sorry for yourself and being in a horrible mood all the time. Get over it! Accept what has happened to you and stop making everybody around you suffer. You have a life to lead! Now lead it!"

"I'm really trying, Mom. Audrey took me to church yesterday. I have God on my side now. I guess I always did, but I'm just now realizing that."

"Well, start behaving like a child of God. He put you here to be a witness. You have so much to offer those around you. You can set a good example for others."

"You are right, Mom. And I am going to try and have a good time tonight. I realize that you really like Ted and I'm sure I will to."

"Thanks, Susie. I really do want you two to like each other."

Chapter 9

"Hi, Ted."

"Hello, Mary."

"Ted, this is my daughter, Susie."

"Hi, Susie. I'm delighted to meet you."

"You, too."

"Have a seat, you two. The waiter should be back soon to take our orders."

"I hope you haven't been waiting too long, Ted. I thought it was best that we meet you here instead of you coming over, because, well, it takes Susie so long to get ready. You know how girls her age are."

"Mom!"

"Susie, you're just as beautiful as your mother said you were."

"Thanks."

"Why don't you tell me something about yourself, Susie?"

"Oh, I'm sure Mom has probably told you everything you need to know. She really loves bragging on me."

" She has, but I know she hasn't told me everything."

"Come on, Susie. Ted just wants to get to know you."

"Mom, you know I really don't want to talk about myself."

"Your mother says you're really doing much better these days."

"What do you mean?"

"Well, she told me about your accident. I'm very sorry."

"Thanks, but I don't want to talk about that."

"Sorry."

"How about you, Ted? Tell me about yourself."

"Well, I work with your mother and I'm very fond of her. I've been divorced for a little over four years."

"Do you have any children?"

"No, I don't."

"I see. I'm really glad you and Mom are able to enjoy each other's company. Thanks for being here for her. I know it's been rough on her the past month or two."

"Susie."

"Mom, it's true."

"Susie, I was glad to be here for her."

"I'm just glad she has someone she can talk to."

"Oh, Susie, your mother says you play baseball. I'm

a big fan of baseball. She says you're very good....Oh, I'm sorry."

"It's alright. I can handle that. I used to not be able to say that. If you would have said something like that a week ago I probably would have left crying, but I'm getting stronger and it's okay. I know you didn't mean to upset me. I'm okay. I still like baseball, even if I can't play right now."

"Well, I just want things to go perfect tonight. I'm glad to have you both here, Mary and Susie."

Chapter 10

On Thursday of the following week, Susie saw her doctor. The swelling in her spinal cord was gone and she could now resume physical therapy. The doctor wanted her to be real careful and to take it slow in physical therapy. He still could not tell her specifics about her recovery and whether she would walk again in six months, a year, or ever. There is always hope, he said. Never give up on something if you really want it. For the next several days, Susie spent every waking moment thinking about her future and how she was going to cope with it. Would she be able to go to college and have a career? Would she be able to have children? Would she ever fall in love and get married? So many unanswered questions. She wasn't sure of any of them. Well, life must go on, she thought. The world doesn't stop for anyone, not even me. So, what am I to do, she thought. In several weeks, school would be starting. She had to be mentally and physically prepared for that. But first and foremost, she kept thinking about Mike. She must call him and get things straightened out with their relationship.

"Mike. Hi, it's Susie!"

"Susie, it's great to hear from you!"

"Mike, I have a lot of things I want to tell you. I'd really like to see you. Do you think you could come over? That is, if you want to?"

"Of course I do. I can't believe you called. I'll be over as soon as I can."

That was the first step. Now she would have to tell him her true feelings. Was she ready for this? She thought so. Oh, God, please let things go okay, she prayed.

"Hi, Mike. Come on in. I'm really glad you could come."

I told you I'd be here when you were ready to talk."

"Well, have a seat. Could I get you something to drink?"

"No, that's okay. I'm fine."

"You sure? It'll only take a minute to get you something."

"Susie, I thought you had some things you wanted to tell me?"

"Oh, yes. Of course I do. I guess I'm a little nervous. I've been doing a lot of thinking the past few days, about my life and future and all. I think I've made things worse than what they really have been."

"Susie, I know these past few months haven't been easy for you. No one expected you to just go on as if nothing happened."

"That's just it, Mike. Everyone did and they still do. Everyone kept telling me that things would get easier – time will make life easier. The funny thing is that everyone who has told me that can still use their legs. How should they know? But you. You came so close to understanding. When I was with you I felt so protected and warm. Mike, I care about you. You've known that."

"I know that I care about you. I was hoping you'd come around."

"I'm sorry I hurt you, Mike."

"No, Susie. I will not have you apologize. You did nothing wrong. I'm the one who made the mistake. You have nothing to apologize for."

"Oh, yes, I do. I have been so selfish the past couple of months. I guess I'm just tired of feeling sorry for myself. I put you through a lot of torment, too. When I saw you with that girl, well, it destroyed me. I thought you had only been feeling sorry for me. But I don't believe that anymore."

"Susie, I never wanted to hurt you."

"I realize that now. Mike, I wasn't really angry at you. I just wanted to strike out at someone. Somehow I thought that would make me feel better."

"Let me help you now. Let's forget everything that's happened and start over. I know we can't forget your paralysis, but I think we can get past that."

"I would really like that, Mike. I really do want that. I feel so close to you."

"I feel close to you, Susie. We really do have a special

relationship and even though we haven't known each other very long, I feel that I want to hold onto what we have."

"Me, too, Mike. Oh, thank you for not losing confidence in me. I certainly did at times. How'd you know I'd be okay?"

"Because you're a strong person. I knew you would call me when you were ready to talk, or at least I hoped you would. I'm really happy you did. I would have really felt horrible if you hadn't."

"I needed some time to get my life back on track. It'll never be the same as it was before the accident. You can't understand how hard that was to accept. I just wanted to wake up and it all be a terrible nightmare, but it wasn't. Maybe now I'll be okay. I realize that I have friends to support me."

"You have great friends, Susie, and a wonderful family. Some people would give anything to be in your shoes. You have a lot to be thankful for."

"I'm thankful to have someone as special as you. I know that."

"Oh, Susie, you're the special one."

Mike walked over to Susie and gently bent his body to meet hers. Their lips met and the feeling after that moment was overwhelming. A magical moment! She wasn't quite sure what to say after that.

"Well, I guess I should be going. I have some things to take care of." Mike was a little overwhelmed himself.

"You don't have to be rushing off so soon, do you?

Mike, you are so incredible. You seem to make things better."

"Susie, how would you like to go out with me again?"

"I'd love to, Mike."

"Terrific! I can't wait! I'll call you tomorrow."

"Bye, Mike."

Days after Mike had kissed Susie, she was still overwhelmed. Mike had actually kissed her! She couldn't believe it! Nothing could upset her now. She knew she was going to survive.

"Hi, Audrey. Come on in. It's great to see you!"

"Boy, Suz, you sure seem happy. That kiss really changed your life, didn't it?"

"Oh, Audrey. I still can't believe he actually kissed me! I'm so crazy about him!"

"Susie, that sounds great! I'm glad that you finally found someone."

"Well, Mike and I are going to start all over again and he did ask me out again."

"Susie, I could kill you! Why didn't you tell me that on the phone?"

"Well, I'm telling you now."

"You two are certainly more than friends, I believe."

"We're just going to take it very slow. He's someone I can really talk to. Of course, so are you."

"Well, I hope so. But I understand, I don't look as good as Mike does."

"Audrey, you are so crazy! I'll always be able to talk to you. That will never change."

"It better not, cause we're best friends for life, right?"

"You bet. And Audrey, I want you to know that I am really sorry about the way I acted, ya know, when I came home from the hospital after my accident. Your friendship means everything to me and you know under normal circumstances I never would have acted that way."

"Susie, I forgave you for that. I understand why you acted that way. I thought we'd forgotten that."

"I know. I just want you to know that I treasure our friendship with my life. I love you, Audrey."

"I feel the same way, Susie. Our friendship is closer than any relationship I've ever had with any of my family. I love you, too."

Ring! Ring!

"Hello?"

"Mike, it's great to hear from you."

"Tonight? No, I'm not doing anything."

"I'd love to! It sounds great!"

"So, you'll be here around seven?"

"I'm so excited!"

"Wear something fancy? Where are we going?"

"Come on. Tell me."

"Okay. I guess I can wait that long."

"Alright, I'll see you tonight. Bye."

"You two going out tonight?"

"Yes, Audrey! Can you believe it? And he said to really dress up. I have no idea where we're going."

"Well, Girl, looks like we're just going to have to go shopping."

"You think we have time? He's picking me up at seven."

"Susie, it's only one o'clock. We have plenty of time."

"Okay. I'll go tell Mom the news and ask her for some money. I have got to look my best for tonight."

"Don't worry. You'll look gorgeous! I promise."

Susie and Audrey went shopping all afternoon. They had such a fun time. They bought Susie a beautiful floral blouse with a matching skirt. When Susie got home she rushed to try it on again for her mother. Her mother could not believe how beautiful and happy Susie appeared. Finally, Susie seemed very happy. Then Mike came and picked Susie up. He wouldn't tell her where they were going. Susie was excited but also anxious to find out what Mike had planned.

"Oh, Mike, I'm still in shock that you brought me here to this dancing club. Even though I can't dance I still love the music. This is a terrific place. Thank you so much for bringing me here."

"Well, I wasn't sure this was right, but I knew you love music, and I thought we could eat and talk and perhaps do some dancing."

"I'm afraid the last part is out."

"No, it isn't."

"Come on! There's no way I can dance, unless you're expecting a miracle."

"Let's go out on the dance floor."

"You're crazy! I'm not going out there. I'd just look silly."

"No, you won't. You may think you can't dance in a wheelchair, but you're wrong. You're coming with me."

"Mike! No!"

Mike pushed Susie out to the dance floor and swirled her around in her wheelchair. Susie was estatic! A wonderful feeling came over her. She felt great! She was actually dancing, maybe not with her legs, but with her spirit and the rest of her body. Mike certainly knew how to make her happy.

"Let's take a break, Susie. I'm getting tired."

"Sure, Mike. I'm having a wonderful time. The best time I've had in a while. Mike, you're great!" Tonight I never would have gone out on that dance floor unless you would have forced me like you did. I really didn't want to at first, but I felt wonderful after I got out there. I couldn't use my legs, but I could move my arms and my wheelchair."

"Susie, you've shown me a lot about life. I guess you've been sort of an inspiration to me."

"Oh, Mike, please. Don't give me so much credit. If the same thing would have happened to you, you'd have survived, too."

"My sister didn't. I wish she could have been as brave as you. I wish I could have been brave, too. I didn't handle her paralysis well. I tried to help, but she always pushed me away. I should have been able to help her. I believe God brought you into my life to help me deal with my sister's suicide. I really believe that. And I'm so glad because you are so special to me now."

"You're special to me, too. I really do care for you, Mike."

"Well, are you ready to get back on the dance floor?"

"Of course, I am!"

Chapter 11

"Hi, Susie! Come on in and get started."

"Great, Mrs. James. I'm feeling much stronger these days. I really think physical therapy is helping. My upper body is so much stronger now. I wish I had had this strength when I was playing baseball. It would have been great!"

Susie was at her physical therapy treatment today and was really excited. Things seemed to be improving for her."

"Susie, I want to start with some new exercises today since you are getting some increased sensation in your legs. I want to concentrate on that today. Ready to get started? "

"I sure am."

Mrs. James began with several unfamiliar exercises today just as she said she would. These exercises were quite challenging for Susie. Susie realized she still had a long road ahead of her, but she was beginning to have hope that someday she would walk right out of that wheelchair.

"You're doing great, Susie! I'm so proud of your hard work! I know things are happening slowly for you, but everyday we're making progress. You have come so far. I know you have had your ups and downs, emotionally, since your accident and I can understand that, but within the past couple of weeks I have noticed a change in you. You seem as though you have accepted your limitations and are coping with them and making small goals for yourself."

"Thanks, Mrs. James. I do feel different. I'm not looking at next year or five years from now. I'm concentrating on today and finding out how I can best cope with my paralysis on a daily basis. I just want to know I can make it through today and now I know I can. Everyday is hard, but with the support of God and my family and friends, I can make it."

"I'm so proud of you, Susie. You have really learned a lot from this whole experience."

Susie was feeling better and performing well in therapy. She had regained some sensation in her legs and could actually wiggle several of her toes. This was great! Two and a half months had passed since her accident and she was now beginning to feel like herself again. She had a new, refreshing relationship with Mike and she had her mother and Audrey by her side. And school. School would be starting back real soon. Susie was somewhat anxious about that. It was going to be so different for her this year. But she was determined to make it a good year. Of course, she would be seeing a lot of students that she hadn't seen since her accident and it would be a bit awkward, but she would make it. It would take a while to get used to being in a wheelchair at school. She just didn't want the teachers or anyone else to feel sorry for her.

Chapter 12

What a lovely day for school to be starting. Susie woke up to a beautiful sunrise and sat up in her bed praying to God to help her through the challenging day ahead. She had a feeling of excitement today added with a little bit of nervousness. She was determined, though, that today was going to be a great day. She had been through such an ordeal this summer, but she had survived. Everything seemed to be going great for her and Mike. He was a very important part of her life now and she was so excited about their future. She was not dwelling on the past anymore. She knew she had great days ahead of her. Susie was ready for school today. This was the beginning of a whole new year filled with promises and successes and she was going to make it through. Yes, she had made it this far and she wasn't going to give up now. Finally, she felt happy after the past few months. She had made it.

"Susie, Honey."
Her mother brought Susie to reality.
"It's time to go to school. Are you ready?"
"Yes, Mom. I'm ready.